Kitty & Me

Henry Holt and Company, LLC
Publishers since 1866
175 Fifth Avenue
New York, New York 10010
mackids.com

Library of Congress Cataloging-in-Publication Data
Kane, Sharon (Sharon Smith), author, illustrator.
Kitty & me / Sharon Smith Kane. — First edition.
pages   cm
Summary: Illustrations and rhyming text portray the friendship between
a girl and her chasing, scratching, purring, and growing Kitty.
ISBN 978-0-8050-9705-4 (hardcover)
[1. Stories in rhyme. 2. Cats—Fiction.] I. Title. II. Title: Kitty and me.
PZ8.3.K12577Kit 2014   [E]—dc23   2013044352

Henry Holt books may be purchased for business or promotional use.
For information on bulk purchases, please contact Macmillan Corporate
and Premium Sales Department at (800) 221-7945 x5442 or by email at
specialmarkets@macmillan.com.

First Edition—2014
The artist used pencil, watercolor, and Prismacolor colored
pencils on Crescent cold-press illustration board to create
the illustrations for this book.

Printed in China by South China Printing Co. Ltd.,
Dongguan City, Guangdong Province

10 9 8 7 6 5 4 3 2 1

Kitty & Me

Written and Illustrated by

Sharon Smith Kane

Christy Ottaviano Books

Henry Holt and Company • New York

*To everyone who loves
a kitty, and to the
kitties who love
them back*

I love Kitty and Kitty loves me.
He comes when I call him . . . usually.

He says "Meow" when he wants to eat.
I feed him some kibble . . . or maybe a treat.

He makes a crunchy noise when he chews,
And when he's full, he likes to snooze.

Whenever Kitty decides to rest,

He'll find a spot he likes the best;

He'll stretch himself out or curl up in a ball

On the couch, or the bed, or the chair in the hall.

He closes his eyes and has kitty dreams
Of mousies or fishies or dancing moon beams.

In the morning while I'm still in bed,
He jumps on my pillow and pats my head.

I love to stroke his soft, warm fur,
And when I do, he loves to purr.

We play fun games around the house,
Like Jump and Pounce and
Catch the Mouse.

He rolls and tumbles as he plays;
I giggle and laugh at his funny ways.

Sometimes Kitty scratches and I say,

"No!
Bad!"

Then he runs and hides 'cause he thinks I'm mad.

But I'm not really mad and my ouch goes away,
So we're friends again and ready to play.

The yard is a jungle where he likes to roam
In the grasses and flowers far from home.
His ears prick up, his eyes open wide
To meet the dangerous world outside.

Kitty sniffs the scents on the summer breeze,
Listens to the sounds of the birds and bees,

And hides under bushes or shady trees.

He crouches and stays as still as a slug,
Then suddenly pounces on a wayward bug.

He'll chase a fly or a bumblebee

And sharpen his claws on the bark of a tree.

Then he likes to follow the garden path
To the place where the birds are taking a bath.
Oh, what fun to watch them splash!
But quick as a wink they're off in a flash.

One day a puppy came
looking for fun.

But Kitty was scared
and wanted to run.

Dashing away, he climbed up a tree. He'd still be stuck there if it weren't for me.

After Kitty's backyard adventure is done,
I hug him and pet him and welcome him home.
He purrs and cuddles and gives me a lick
And meows, "Hey, I'm hungry!
    Please feed me quick!"

So I give him his dinner and then I have mine,
And soon with full tummies, we're both feeling fine.

While I read him a story or little rhyme,
Kitty listens and does his grooming time.
He cleans his paw, then wipes his face,
And licks his fur 'till it's all in place.

And when he's finished, all fluffy and clean,
He's the handsomest kitty I've ever seen!

And when I go to bed at night,
Snuggle in, turn off the light,
Kitty comes to keep me warm,
And protect me, too, from any harm.
It's a promise he likes to keep
And I hear him purr as I fall asleep.

I love Kitty and Kitty loves me . . .
And that's the way it will always be.